For Francesca and Luke Brewster
—B. H.

For my parents
—T. L. M.

Henry Holt and Company, *Publishers since 1866*
Henry Holt® is a registered trademark of Macmillan Publishing Group, LLC
175 Fifth Avenue, New York, NY 10010 • mackids.com

Text copyright © 2018 by Bridget Heos
Illustrations copyright © 2018 by Trenton McBeath
All rights reserved.

Library of Congress Cataloging-in-Publication Data
Names: Heos, Bridget, author. | McBeth, T.L., illustrator.
Title: Stegothesaurus / Bridget Heos ; pictures by T.L. McBeth.
Description: First edition. | New York : Henry Holt and Company, 2018. |
Summary: Stegothesaurus has little in common with his fellow dinosaurs
until he meets an allosaurus that seems as hungry for synonyms as he is.
Identifiers: LCCN 2017041225 | ISBN 978-1-250-13488-2 (hardcover)
Subjects: CYAC: English language—Synonyms and antonyms—Fiction. |
Stegosaurus—Fiction. | Allosaurus—Fiction. | Dinosaurs—Fiction. | Brothers—Fiction.
Classification: LCC PZ7.H4118 Ste 2018 | DDC [E]—dc23
LC record available at https://lccn.loc.gov/2017041225

Our books may be purchased in bulk for promotional, educational, or business use. Please contact your local bookseller or the Macmillan
Corporate and Premium Sales Department at
(800) 221-7945 ext. 5442 or by e-mail at MacmillanSpecialMarkets@macmillan.com.

First edition, 2018
The illustrations for this book were created using graphite pencil and Photoshop.
Printed in China by RR Donnelley Asia Printing Solutions Ltd., Dongguan City, Guangdong Province
1 3 5 7 9 10 8 6 4 2

STEGOTHESAURUS

Bridget Heos
illustrated by T. L. McBeth

Henry Holt and Company
New York

Once upon a time, there were three dinosaurs.

A stegosaurus.

Another stegosaurus.

And a . . .

stego*thesaurus*.

Hello!
Greetings!
Salutations!

He was a little different from his brothers.

Stegothesaurus knew lots of words and used them to describe everything he saw, like the clouds, for example.

Fluffy, fleecy, feathery.

As the dinosaurs trekked across the desert
looking for something to eat,
a mountain appeared in the distance.

"Big," said the first stegosaurus.
"Big," said the second stegosaurus.

"Gargantuan,
gigantic,
Goliath,"
said Stegothesaurus.

The sun rose.

"Hot," said the first stegosaurus.
"Hot," said the second stegosaurus.

**"Blazing,
blistering,
broiling,"**

said Stegothesaurus.

At long last, the brothers found some shrubs to eat.
"Yummy," said the first stegosaurus.
"Yummy," said the second stegosaurus.

"Savory,
succulent,
scrumptious,"
said Stegothesaurus.

Satisfied and sleepy, the three dinosaurs
decided to take a rest. Little did they know . . .

an allosaurus was lurking nearby.

Suddenly, it bounded out from the grove of trees.

"Scary!" said the first stegosaurus.
"Scary!" said the second stegosaurus.

And both ran away.

But Stegothesaurus was too busy
thinking of all the words that
described the allosaurus:

"F-f-f-frightening, formidable, fearsome."

The allosaurus opened its mouth, baring its teeth, which Stegothesaurus couldn't help but notice were

"p-p-p-pointy, piercing, peaked."

But rather than chomping down on Stegothesaurus,
the allosaurus looked at him and said,

Hulking,
hefty,
humongous.

As it turned out, she wasn't an allosaurus after all.
She was an allo*thesaurus*.

The two dinothesauruses passed the day
describing all that they saw.

After a day of adventure, it was dinnertime.
As Stegothesaurus nibbled on shrubs, he asked,

"Well," Allothesaurus answered. "One day . . .

. . . I ate a stegothesaurus."

At that moment, only one word popped
into Stegothesaurus's head:
Not *trot*, *traipse*, or *travel*.
Not *skitter*, *scramble*, or *scoot*, but . . .

And he ran and ran
until he caught up with his brothers,

who were very relieved to see him.

"Hug," said the first.
"Hug," said the second.

"Snuggle, cuddle, squeeze,"
said Stegothesaurus.

~~The Finale~~
~~The Conclusion~~
~~The Closing~~
The End

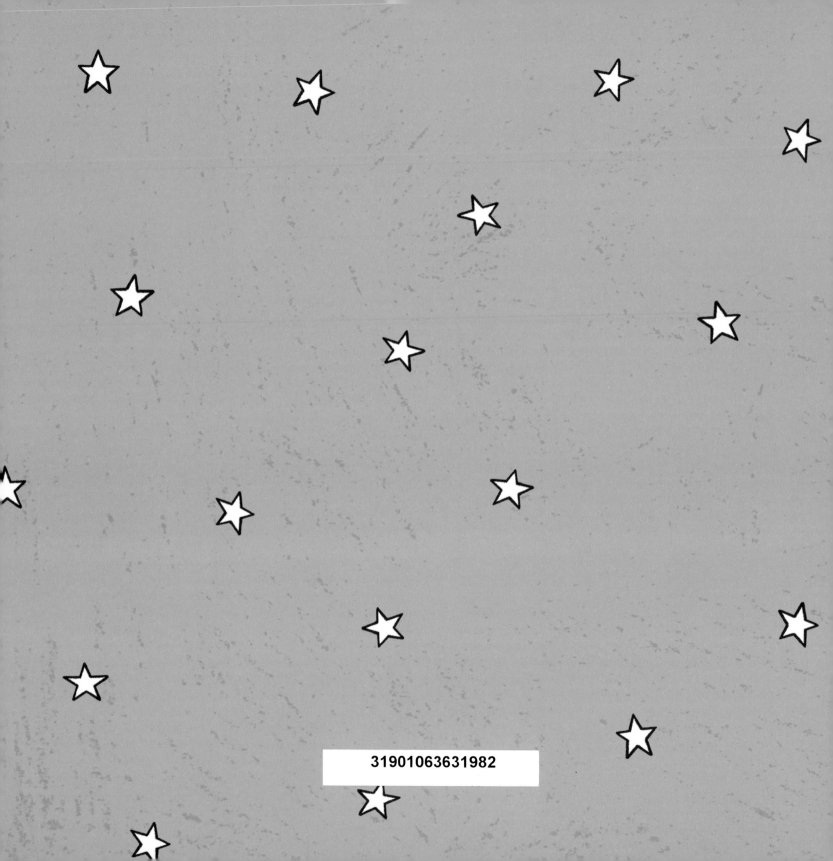